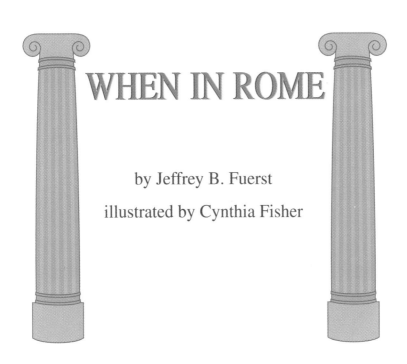

WHEN IN ROME

by Jeffrey B. Fuerst

illustrated by Cynthia Fisher

Scott Foresman

Editorial Offices: Glenview, Illinois • New York, New York
Sales Offices: Reading, Massachusetts • Duluth, Georgia
Glenview, Illinois • Carrollton, Texas • Menlo Park, California

Have you ever heard that expression "When in Rome, do as the Romans do"? It means you should follow the rules, wherever you are. I learned it the hard way.

It was my Uncle Kronos's fault—sort of. He's not really my uncle. I just call him that. He works with my Dad in the records department at the hospital—when he's not inventing neat stuff. He comes to our house for holiday dinners.

It happened last Thanksgiving.

I picked up a large piece of turkey with my fingers.

When I dunked the meat into cranberry sauce
in a bowl in the middle of the table, Uncle
Kronos winced.

"You eat like a barbarian!" he said.

"How do they eat?" I shot back.

"You'll find out soon enough."

"Dessert for breakfast, I hope!" Before I got out
a snicker, I found myself in ancient Rome, two
thousand years ago.

Did I mention that Uncle Kronos's latest gadget
is a remote-controlled time machine?

Uncle Kronos had sent me back in time before.
So I knew I'd come back in one piece . . . probably.

I landed in the middle of a big party. There was so much food. Musicians! Dancers! Jugglers! People were laughing—until they saw me.

The guy in charge clapped his hands once, loudly. The music stopped. The juggling balls dropped. The dancers tripped. All eyes turned toward me. They stared. They glared. I could tell they were dismayed. But why?

"Who, or what, do we have here?" said the head guy. I figured he must be the host.

"From the way he's dressed," said a woman with freckles on her cheek, "I'd guess he's a barbarian from the North."

"But he's wearing a purple stripe," said another guest. "That's the mark of a noble person."

The man who said this looked just like my school-bus driver, Sal.

"Then he must be the leader of the barbarians," said the host.

I didn't deny it. After all, I *did* lead off the batting order for our championship baseball team. I have the trophy to prove it.

"Then let our royal visitor eat with us," said the host. He was making an exception to the usual dining rules of ancient Rome. Back then, kids ate sitting on stools in front of the adults.

The host led me to a three-person dining couch called a *triclinia*. The guests were lying down and eating.

My first reaction was, "No slouching at the dinner table!" I'd heard Uncle Kronos say that a million times. But I didn't say it out loud. I didn't want to be rude. You know, "When in Rome. . . ."

A bunch of waiters swarmed over me like moths at a candle convention. One took off my shoes. Another crowned me with an olive-leaf headband. A third washed my hands—*and feet*—in perfume. I winced. I smelled like my mom on New Year's Eve!

I was hungry. After all, I hadn't eaten for two thousand years. (Ha-ha!)

There wasn't a fork in sight. So I dug in—just like everyone else—with my hands! Thanks, Uncle Kronos! Ancient Rome is my kind of place.

It was tasty food too. I couldn't stop eating, until I heard the whispering. Quiet at first, it grew louder and louder.

"Nobleman?" cried the Freckle Lady. She was sitting on my couch. "He eats like a barbarian. He's using all five fingers—of his left hand. Everyone knows one uses only three on the right hand."

She held up her right hand, tucking the pinky and ring finger into her palm.

"I apologize," I said, my face as red as a ripe tomato. "I didn't realize this was a formal occasion."

She forgave me. Then she sneezed.

I didn't know if that was part of ancient Roman etiquette or if she just had an itchy nose. To be safe, I said "Bless you!" in my loudest, most sincere voice. You can't imagine the chaos that followed!

"What kind of rude remark is that?" said bus driver Sal's twin.

Even my host, who never seemed to be without a smile, frowned at me.

"Congratulations are in order when someone sneezes," he scolded. "Be polite, and raise your cap to my guest."

Now I was dismayed. Congratulations? For a sneeze? Ancient Romans, as I learned, believed that sneezing was a good thing. They thought it got rid of illnesses inside the body.

That was the wackiest custom I'd ever heard of—until what happened next.

Waiters gave each guest a bowl filled with a sweet-smelling soup. I dipped in my spoon (they did have spoons) and slurped.

People began to giggle. The giggles turned to guffaws. Then everyone cracked up. They pointed at me.

I was about to say that where I come from, pointing is rude. But I was in ancient Rome. *Now* what had I done wrong?

Maybe they drink soup straight from the bowl, I thought. So I did.

Wrong! The howling that followed was loud enough to cause deafness.

"My young friend," said the host, trying not to bust a gut. "If you're thirsty, we'll give you a drink. But that bowl has water scented with rose petals. We wash our hands in it between courses."

P-tooey! I winced at the thought of what I'd just drunk.

"You may wipe your greasy fingers on a piece of bread," explained the Freckle Lady.

She showed me the proper technique. Then she gave me a slice. Must I? Using bread as a napkin, I have to admit, repulsed even me.

Bus driver Sal's look-alike came to my rescue. "Or you may use your 'serviette.'" He pointed to the cloth next to me.

That was more like it. But unfolded, my napkin was as big as a towel! I was confused. Did they expect me to take a bath *during* the meal?

That's when I suddenly let out with a burp. It was a full-bodied "BRRRAAAP!" It probably broke all loudness records.

Total silence followed. I was so embarrassed. I tried to hide under the pillows of my couch. The host of the party ran over. I was sure I'd be asked to leave. Or worse!

But instead he gave me a hug!

"You're welcome," he said. "I'm glad you enjoyed our food."

In ancient Rome, you see, burping after eating was considered the height of good manners.

Wow! These strange manners were making my head swim.

"Uncle Kronos," I said under my breath, "I get the point." He often watched my trips on a special TV.

"I see food on your plate," said my host. He frowned.

Now what had I done wrong? Was there an ancient Roman law against leftovers?

I wanted to keep eating the wonderful food. But my stomach was more stuffed than our Thanksgiving turkey.

"Sorry. I'm full," I sighed.

"Wrap up what's left in your napkin," said my host. "Take it home to your barbarian subjects."

Yum! An ancient Roman doggie bag!

"It's a very popular dish," he continued, "sow's paunch."

"What?!"

"The stomach of a female pig," explained the Freckle Lady. "It's my favorite too."

That's what I'd had seconds—and thirds—of? My face turned green!

"But I can't take this home," I cried, "It's . . ."

"You refuse to take food from my table?" my host cried. "I have never been so insulted! You are indeed an unmannered barbarian!"

"I told you so," said Freckle Lady.

I didn't see any way out, so I agreed.

"You're right. I am a barbarian."

"Then be gone," said my host.

And with that, I was whisked back to the present. PLOP! I dropped back into my chair, just as Mom was passing out the pumpkin pie.

"You see?" Uncle Kronos chuckled. "It is just as I told you. You *do* eat like a barbarian."

"Anything you say," I said, "as long as I get some pumpkin pie."

"It does go well after sow's paunch," laughed Uncle Kronos. "Very well!"